The Cupcake
Chronicles

Also by Patricia Carragon

Journey to the Center of My Mind, Rogue Scholars Press, 2005

Urban Haiku and More, Illustrated by William L. Hays, Fierce Grace Press, 2010

Innocence, Finishing Line Press, 2017

It is a testament to her vivacious spirit that Patricia Carragon would think to personify cupcakes as a device to chronicle quotidian activities and as a mode to assuage the anxieties of her daily jaunts. Tasty diary entries mingle humor and contemplative musings in a way that not only tantalizes the tongue but stimulates all of the sensory receptors, as her imagery erupts from the page to entice one's very soul.

— ALISON ROSS, PUBLISHER AND EDITOR OF
CLOCKWISE CAT

The Cupcake Chronicles is a tasty confection. Ms. Carragon has whipped up a batter of metaphor, mysticism, and whimsy, sprinkled with the right words, layered with meaning, baked to perfection and topped with a sweet frosting of fable. Warning, this is not for poetry aficionados on a diet, these prose poems are very filling. They will satisfy the hunger for delicious and flavorful writing but will have you standing in line wanting seconds.

— PETER V. DUGAN, NASSAU COUNTY POET
LAUREATE 2016 – 2018

The Cupcake Chronicles is an imaginative fable that explores what would happen if your afternoon treat were to suddenly come to life. A quick read, and you may never look at cupcakes in quite the same way.

— FRANCINE WITTE, AUTHOR OF *NOT ALL FIRES
BURN THE SAME*

The Cupcake Chronicles

Patricia Carragon

POETS WEAR PRADA • Hoboken, New Jersey

The Cupcake Chronicles

Poets Wear Prada
533 Bloomfield Street, 2nd Floor
Hoboken, NJ 07030
http://pwpbooks.blogspot.com/

First North American Publication 2017
First Mass Market Edition 2017

Grateful acknowledgment is made to *Red Fez*, *Symmetry Pebbles*, and *Tattoosday (A Tattoo Blog)*, where some of these stories originally appeared.

The front cover is inspired by one for an 1898 edition of Lewis Carroll a.k.a. Charles Lutwidge Dodgson's *Alice's Adventures in Wonderland* and incorporates Alice from one of Sir John Tenniel's 42 illustrations "You're nothing but a pack of cards!" and words she finds on a very small cake.

ISBN-13: 978-0-9979811-7-9
ISBN-10: 0-9979811-7-2

Printed in the U.S.A.

Front Cover Design: Roxanne Hoffman
Back Cover Author Photo: Mira Batra
Interior Author Photo: Flash Rosenberg

For my niece and nephew with love

Table of Contents

Friday Afternoon, March 16, 2018 / 3

Friday Evening Rush Hour, March 16, 2018 / 4

Saturday Morning Before Eleven, January 5, 2019 / 6

Saturday Afternoon Around Three, April 6, 2019 / 7

Monday Evening Before Seven Thirty, May 4, 2020 / 8

Wednesday Morning at Nine, November 4, 2020 / 10

Thursday Evening After Seven, July 22, 2021 / 12

Tuesday After School, February 22, 2022 / 14

Friday After Midnight, September 16, 2022 / 16

Saturday After Midnight, August 5, 2023 / 18

Tuesday Morning at Seven Fifty-Nine, October 22, 2024 / 20

Sunday Evening After Six Thirty, June 1, 2025 / 22

Friday at Bedtime, December 13, 2030 / 24

Acknowledgments / 27

About the Author / 29

The Cupcake Chronicles

Friday Afternoon

Something happened at work today. I saw cupcakes — the size of hobbits — parading the halls. With swinging arms and marching legs to match their lemon, orange, vanilla, cinnamon, red-velvet, pumpkin, angel- and devil's-food bodies, they had fluffy buttercream heads, every shade and flavor of a baker's rainbow. Some had chocolate jimmies, others white sprinkles or multicolored nonpareils. Some were seasonal, some had nuts, some were topped by a single maraschino cherry. The rest were plain. No one seemed to notice them but me.

The afternoon meeting in the conference room was at four, and I was hungry. A cupcake with thick mint-green frosting sat down beside me. I thought I heard it say what sounded like "Eat me." It leaned in closer, but I slid back, fearful its green buttercream would grace the right shoulder of my white sweater. It seemed this cupcake's mission was to feed me. Quite hungry, I started to squirm uneasily in my seat. Coworkers asked if I was OK.

Then the green cupcake quietly left the room.

Confectionary madness took mass transit home. I walked into a crowded subway car filled with cupcake commuters of every racial and ethnic variety. I felt like Gulliver underground. I sat between two white-laced, chocolate-iced, cream-filled devil's-food cakes — one read *The New York Times*, the other *amNew York*. Across from me was a petite freckled Lady Baltimore, stinking of sherry, rocking to the music from her headphones. Two red-velvet males shared a pole and joked about their jobs and the latest cream dos topped with those ever-so-trendy maraschino cherries.

Sitting diagonally from me was a mother vanilla cupcake with three screaming lemon-cream-top kids. The kids were arguing over who had the most Hello Kitty sprinkles. A bite-size version of their mother wailed from a stroller. An aging Yankee Doodle with his Hostess Twinkie wife complained about the noise and moved to the other end of the car but then hesitated to sit by a homeless applesauce cupcake with dirty-beige frosting.

A badly bitten banana nut passed by, begging for spare change. My mint-green friend from work was now seated next to me and nodding off. I shrunk away though I was craving to lick that mint icing. Loud snoring prompted snickers from our fellow passengers. I started to panic and got up to push my way through waves of buttercream to escape at the next stop.

Instead of returning to humanity, I was on a platform surrounded by baked confections. I ran to the nearest stairwell to flee this madness. As I ran, my heart pumping, faster and faster, I passed a shiny aluminum-plated pillar. I gasped, blinked twice, halted by my reflection — a hobbit-size vanilla cupcake, topped by a spiral of strawberry buttercream strewn with white sprinkles, stared back at me.

OMG, I was one of *them!*

Saturday Morning Before Eleven

Over the weekend all the cupcakes came down with the flu, and all the cupcake shops in New York were quarantined for health violations. I rushed over to the Sweet Dreams Bakeshop, hoping they had remained open. Behind windows now adorned with menacing signs, cupcakes rested in baby-doll beds — their buttercream heads flattened against tiny pink pillows. Teeny thermometers dangled from their mouths. The cupcakes were so sick, their frosted heads had turned gray.

The bakers and clerks, dressed as doctors and nurses, were reading from a gigantic medical cookbook, on how to care for their patients. Confusion reigned and seemed the only prognosis.

I watched from the other side of the glass, every taste bud urging me to lick that gray frosting.

Saturday Afternoon Around Three

The wedding was high society — sumptuous and lavish beyond dreams. I was neither the lucky bride nor an unlucky bridesmaid — just a casual acquaintance of the groom. Flowers of every exotic origin decorated the tables and marble staircase. The food was catered by an upscale New York restaurant, importing the skills of one of the finest chefs of Europe. It was more perfect than perfection. It was also distinctly different from your customary millionaire's reception. Even the design of the wedding cake was unique, consisting of twenty tiers of cupcakes decorated with gorgeous lilac and white buttercream rose petals. The top tier had two cupcakes — one done up as yang for the groom, the other as yin for the bride.

When the bride and groom were ready for the cake-cutting ceremony, the yin cupcake threw a fit, kicking its yang mate off the top tier. The ejected yang cupcake landed, icing face down, onto the bride's pristine white Vera Wang gown. The groom laughed so hard, he soon learned to regret it. Other cupcakes joined the ensuing fray. An unfortunate slapstick of icing and mashed cake smeared the guests below.

The wedding couple ended their vows in divorce.

Monday Evening Before Seven Thirty

I couldn't resist temptation. Before me was a tray of devil's food and vanilla cupcakes topped with delectable pink buttercream clouds. I wanted one of each. The clerk packed my selections in a box and then carefully placed the box into a plastic bag. I paid the clerk three and a half dollars for two cupcakes — and now they were mine.

I carried my precious cargo home, proudly, knowing my teeth would soon be sinking into those delectable pink buttercream clouds before biting into moist cake. But then I realized that eating two whole cupcakes, all at once, might do a number on my diet. An obvious solution would be to slice one of the cupcakes in half, eating half today and saving half for tomorrow. The day after tomorrow, I'd start on the second cupcake, repeating the process. My pleasure would extend four whole days!

Opening the box, I removed the devil's food cupcake and placed it on a paper plate. I grabbed the cake knife, ready to execute my will to eat just half. I heard a scream. The cupcake shook in terror. Little arms and legs wriggled in fear. The knife dropped to the floor. Tears in my eyes, I ran from the kitchen, swearing that as long as I had teeth I'd never touch another cupcake again.

Wednesday Morning at Nine

Armageddon paid New York a brief visit. It was not Friday the Thirteenth, nor was Mercury in Retrograde. Chocolate chip cookies had arrived at the Sweet Dreams Bakeshop. Several cupcakes, feeling threatened by the appearance of *illegal alien* confections on their shelves, swiftly mobilized units, putting aside past differences. The bakers and clerks tried to negotiate peace, promising the cookies were there to help promote business, not to compete with or diminish the significance of the cupcakes. But the two head cupcakes wanted war and got it, although the majority voted against it. *Something must have happened to the voting machines in the red section of the store!*

Warmonger cakes attacked the cookies, tossing them like frisbees. Cookie chunks and crumbs scattered everywhere, across the counter tops and floors. Some peace-loving cupcakes formed a Red Cross unit and tried to rescue the broken cookies. Others marched against brutality. A cupcake militia was rushed in with mini rolling pins to keep the peace.

Pastel and chocolate frosting splattered across walls, floors, counters, and windows. Battered cupcakes joined the ranks of broken cookies. Soon the shop looked like the result of a bad pillow fight or too much confetti at a birthday party. The bakers and clerks ducked behind one of the counters, called 9-1-1, and waited and waited and waited for a response.

Meanwhile anarchy happened. There was a split within the cupcake administration. The two head cupcakes were unceremoniously ousted into a garbage bin, and peace returned to the Sweet Dreams Bakeshop. Harmony was declared between the surviving chocolate chip cookies and cupcakes.

The bakers and clerks, however, were not too pleased — hours wasted calling for help, placed on hold only to be disconnected, a day's business lost, and now a major clean up tonight to get ready for tomorrow morning's reopening.

Thursday Evening After Seven

He knew his head wasn't in the clouds. Like the cotton fillers inside aspirin bottles, clouds were generally visions in white. Most of these puffy mounds were shades of cotton candy. He spotted a chocolate-brown mound among the pastels. Choosing the chocolate, he collapsed into it as if it were a mattress. He had imagined clouds smelling moist, but his smelled sweet. It reminded him of freshly made frosting, waiting in a bowl, ready for finger tasting.

His stomach grew eyes larger than the ones on his face. Once again he was "little Johnny" back in his mom's Bayside kitchen. How he loved those Duncan Hines cupcakes, despite Mom's claim that they could never duplicate the ultimate delight of the Ebinger's or Cushman's from her girlhood Flatbush days. She had just finished frosting the cupcakes and was handing him one.

He was ready to bite into the thick rich chocolate frosting, but a persistent tapping on his shoulder interrupted him.

He woke up with his face pressed against the window. The steward smiled and apologized, holding a tray with one chocolate-frosted chocolate cupcake. It looked just like the one from his dream! A chorus of somewhat inebriated folks in First Class broke out into an off-key version of "Happy Birthday." A plastic number 40 was buried in the frosting.

———

Later I kissed him and confessed to having arranged his little surprise, with the airline. He wasn't thrilled by the advertisement of his chronological advancement. He had felt embarrassed, even lost his appetite for his beloved dessert.

Had altitude mixed with alcohol tampered his mind? Or was it just age catching up with him?

Tuesday After School

A little banana nut cupcake was asking his mother profound questions:

"When a cupcake dies, does it go to Heaven, Hell, or nowhere like some humans? Or does it get reincarnated?"

The mother cupcake answered, "It goes into a human's mouth and travels down the esophagus until it reaches the stomach and dies. Humans use us up to fuel their energy. We make our way into the next world when they go to the bathroom."

"Does that mean we end up in the toilet?"

"Yes, sweetie. That's life. We are here to look delicious and to please the sweet tooth of the human race." The mother cupcake sighed, hoping her mini offspring would get bored and change the subject. She saw me pass the counter. She had a premonition that the end was near.

The little cupcake was not satisfied by his mother's wisdom. He continued to badger her, repeating, "Mommy, that's not fair!"

"Life isn't meant to be fair, but I'm sure we'll be richly rewarded in the afterworld."

—∞—

My eyes surveyed the mother and son cupcakes. They were the last banana nut cupcakes in the shop. I couldn't decide whether I wanted the angel- or devil's-food cupcakes, on the left side of the case, instead. My mind was in a quandary.

—∞—

The child cupcake was angry: "Mommy, I want to eat the humans."

"No, dear. We don't speak this way because we might have to work out our problems the next time around."

"Mommy, why not? No matter how hard we try, we still end up in the toilet. Do we go to Heaven or Hell from there? Or do we just come back as cupcakes, again, in this same shop?"

The mother couldn't answer before a hand slid the glass door behind her open. The hand reached for their tray and removed them. They were both packed in a box. The little cupcake was too scared to speak. The mother prayed.

—∞—

I left the Sweet Dreams Bakeshop, clutching my cakebox, feeling blessed.

15

Friday After Midnight

It was the end of the world. All the cupcakes had vanished overnight. All the bakeshops had stopped making them. In every cookbook, all cupcake recipe pages were now blank. All depictions, in every media — art, music, theater, dance, film, literature, TV — had disappeared. Every artifact — gone. All memory of cupcakes died but mine. I cried all day until I fell asleep that night.

The following morning I felt bloated as I rose from my bed. I passed the mirror and noticed how voluptuous my boobs looked. I headed for the fridge and raided the pickle and peanut butter jars. I decided to add garlic and paprika on a scoop of vanilla ice cream. My appetite craved the most unusual combinations.

My period was a month and a half late. It was time to call my gynecologist.

The sonogram showed multiple fetuses. The doctor pointed out perfectly formed hands and feet, but the heads and torsos seemed odd — perhaps too early in development.

The doctor went quiet for a few moments. Then she

smiled and said, "Congratulations, you're having a baker's dozen!"

Saturday After Midnight

I dreamt I saw God. It was in every flavor imaginable, including the icing. It sat on a throne of sugar cubes. Like Amun-Ra, it held the staff of life in one hand — a large golden spoon — and the symbol of eternal life in the other — the whisk. The cherubim consisted of the world's cupcakes. They had wings dusted in confectioner's sugar and wore rock-candy halos. They carried buttercream florets. Hallelujahs and hosannas resonated Heaven's hallway of chocolate kisses, nuts, sprinkles, maraschino cherries, and star-shaped sugar candies. A fusion of cake batter, sweet cream and butter, cinnamon and brown sugar, cocoa and vanilla beans perfumed the air. It was intoxicating, and I was experiencing *true religion.*

I stood in the presence of God, Master Baker of all things creamy and yummy. I did not see any form of human life, past or present, amid the grand hallway, but I did not care. I may have been dead, but I didn't mind. I was on such a high that I grabbed one of the cupcake angels and bit off its head.

Bingo! Judgment Day arrived. God saw what happened and condemned the heathen human, with the telltale icing on her face and hands, to Hell.

Buttercream cherubim booed me, giving me the smeared thumbs down, before throwing me down the nearest shaft.

———∞———

I woke up with an aching head, bad heartburn, and a ten-pound weight gain.

Tuesday Morning at Seven Fifty-Nine

Something went wrong with the oven thermostat. Instead of being set at the normal three hundred and fifty degrees, the thermostat was elevated beyond five hundred. Human error wasn't to blame. The poor oven couldn't control what was happening within its immense belly. It cried for help, but the bakers were on their coffee break. Not yet eight, it was too early for the clerks to have arrived. The oven groaned, sweating profusely. The bakers were oblivious, sipping their java while joking about their love lives. One baker named Lisa had her headphones on. Her cell phone sensed the terrible situation in the kitchen and broke away leaving white earphones dangling from its owner's ears. Lisa turned to see her phone jumping up and down and banging on the kitchen door. She had never before noticed that her iPhone 13 had arms and legs. The text message "Help, the oven is overheated" flashed across its screen. But it was too late.

The shop exploded. Instead of an inferno, a garden of earthly buttercream delights replaced the Sweet Dreams Bakeshop. Surrounding a bedazzled and weary oven were freshly baked cupcakes being iced by yesterday's batch. There was no need for the bakers to return as the cupcakes had become self-sufficient. Besides, the bakers were opening up a new restaurant down the block. They had emptied their coffee cups and moved on.

After frosting the freshly baked cupcakes, yesterday's cupcakes danced the "Ring-Around-the Rosie" and played hide-and-seek under bell-shaped flowers. It looked like a scene painted by Bosch. Even the cell phone joined in, singing its streaming songs, before its owner ran back to grab it.

I was on my way to work and cried when I saw my favorite shop gone. I shrugged my shoulders, depressed amongst the revelry. Then a cupcake topped with lilac buttercream sauntered over. It held out two black binders, offering them to me. One binder contained all the magic recipes that gave cupcakes life and their heavenly taste. The other, a medical cookbook, contained recipes on how to care for sick cupcakes.

I thanked the lilac-topped cupcake for the two cookbooks and waved goodbye. I returned home and decided to call out sick.

I had a different agenda and a brand new future to consider.

Sunday Evening After Six Thirty

I am on my way to visit the master bakers of the world. I have boarded my private jet and buckled-up in my comfortable chair. Since the demise of the original Sweet Dreams Bakeshop, the magical recipes have dramatically increased my wealth, surpassing my expectations. Who could have imagined that a struggling working girl without prior financial know-how or commercial baking experience would become the CEO of her own cupcake company?

The magical cookbooks contained a history of traditions, garnered over the centuries, from wizards, priests, and shamans. I was able to conjure spells to improve the recipes used by the original Sweet Dreams Bakeshop bakers, who now ran the Blue River restaurant down the block. A chocolate fudge cupcake told me that Lisa, one of the old bakers, discovered these cookbooks in a thrift shop in the East Village but was only interested in quick money. She had no interest in the eclectic writings in the backs of the books. Several scholarly cupcakes, seeing my potential, assisted me in breaking the ancient code on how the Egyptian goddesses kept their supermodel figures. I also learned sacred chants for keeping the cupcakes healthy and fresh.

One morning, at dawn, a week before the full moon, I secretly performed a diet spell in the shop. Since then no one has put on a pound from eating my cupcakes!

Customers line up outside the door and around the block. I've expanded my shop into the one next door and hired more employees to keep up with the demand. I love the profit and my reflection in the mirror. I've kept my discovery secured in a vault until now. But now I am ready to share my discovery to promote peace throughout the world!

My thirteen cupcake kids are with me. I married that rich chocolate treat who used to be Johnny, my human boyfriend. Johnny loved chocolate so much that he got to be what he always wanted — he morphed into his favorite dessert.

After all, you are what you eat.

Friday at Bedtime

"And so they lived *sort of* happily ever after." The mother chocolate cupcake closed the book and kissed her daughter's marshmallow head goodnight.

"So now what do we do with the human we bought at the bakeshop today? Would it squirm if we cut it in half? Mommy, you made humans sound so real!"

The mother cupcake smiled.

"No sweetie, it won't. The world is a nicer place without humans in charge. Humans get too hungry for power and greed. As you know, war is now extinct. Humans are better off as desserts. A little sugar goes a long way. I could tell you stories about when I was your age, but now it's getting past your bedtime."

"OK, Mommy. Goodnight!"

The mother cupcake closed the bedroom door. The child grinned, enjoying her taste of freedom. She had her own magic hidden away inside the nightstand drawer — within a small box from the Sweet Dreams Bakeshop. The laughing cupcake removed the treasure from the box. Her mouth enlarged to engulf her special treat.

———⊷———

I saw her teeth and screamed.

Acknowledgments

The author extends her thanks to the following publications where these stories, in slightly different formats and under different titles, originally appeared:

"Saturday Afternoon Around Three, April 6, 2019"	*Symmetry Pebbles*, January 29, 2011
"Wednesday Morning at Nine, November 4, 2020"	*Red Fez*, Issue #37, August 2011
"Thursday Evening After Seven, July 22, 2021"	*Symmetry Pebbles*, Alt. Valentine Selection, February 14, 2011
"Thursday After School, February 22, 2022"	*Red Fez*, Issue #37, August 2011
"Friday After Midnight, September 16, 2022"	*Tattoosday (A Tattoo Blog)*, The Tattooed Poets Project, April 2, 2011
"Saturday After Midnight, August 5, 2023"	*Symmetry Pebbles*, Issue #2, November 2011
"Sunday Evening After Six Thirty, June 1, 2025"	*Symmetry Pebbles*, Alt. Valentine Session, February 14, 2011
"Friday at Bedtime, December 13, 2030"	*Red Fez*, Issue #34, May 2011

Her videographed readings from *The Cupcake Chronicles* can by found on Bam Bam Slam Video (December 2007) and on YouTube (Poets Wear Prada Channel, January 2008).

About the Author

Brooklynite Patricia Carragon, a lover of buttercream frosting, all things chocolate, cute cuddly kitties, and everything pink and girly, is the author of *Journey to the Center of My Mind* (Rogue Scholars Press, 2005), *Urban Haiku and More* (Fierce Grace Press, 2010), and *Innocence* (Finishing Line Press, 2017). When she's not cooking up some magic in her kitchen, you'll most likely find her carting a tray of baked treats to a poetry reading. A frequently featured writer on the New York City poetry circuit, she also hosts her own Brooklyn-based monthly reading series, Brownstone Poets. She is the editor in chief for the annual anthology of the same name.

Her poetry and flash fiction have been published in numerous anthologies, most recently *Maintenant 6: A Journal of Contemporary Dada Writing & Art* (Three Rooms Press, 2012); *Mom Egg Review*, Vol. #15 (Half Shell Press, 2017, ed. Marjorie Tessler); *Palabras Luminosas (Luminous Words)*, ANYDSWPE Anthology Series, Volume 3 (Rogue Scholars Press, 2016); and *One Hundred Voices*, Vol. II (Centum Press, 2017).

Widely published in literary journals, both print and online, her work has appeared in *Avocet, Big City Lit, Bear Creek Haiku, Best Poem, Boog City, Chantarelle's Notebook, CLWN WR, Clockwise Cat, Danse Macabre, Drunk Monkeys, First Literary Review-East, Inertia, LIPS, Levure littéraire, Long Island Quarterly, Mad Hatters' Review, Möbius: The Poetry Magazine, Panoply, poeticdiversity, Tribe Magazine, The Toronto Quarterly, Word Salad*

Poetry Magazine, Yellow Chair Review, among other places.

Patricia is an active member of Brevitas, a group fiercely dedicated to short poems, as well as the PEN Women's Literary Workshop and Tamarind. She is one of the executive editors for *Home Planet News Online.*

For more information, please visit her online at http://brownstonepoets.blogspot.com and http://patriciacarragon8.wordpress.com.

ABOUT THE TYPE

Text for this book is set in Bookman Old Style, designed by Ong Chong Wah (b. 1955) for Monotype and released in 1990. The Malaysian-born graphic and font designer studied and worked in England, mostly in advertising prior to Monotype. His credits also include the ever-popular Footlight (Monotype) and Ocean Sans (Adobe) among a total of nine type families.

Ong's Bookman Old Style is characterized by the near-vertical stress of its face, heavy type color, wide letters, and the somewhat taller lowercase characteristic of hymn and classic children's books. Ong based his digitized design on various 1960s and 1970s phototypesetting revivals of Alexander Phemister's classic Old Style Antique (circa 1858) cut for the Miller and Richard foundry in Edinburgh, Scotland as a "modern" recasting of the Caslon typeface cut by William Caslon in the 1720s.

Despite its "old style" moniker and look — or perhaps because of it — Ong's design continues to prevail. Title designer Victoria Vaus selected Bookman Old Style for the main title of the 1999 film *Election*, a high school comedy starring Matthew Broderick and Reese Witherspoon, directed by Alexander Payne. Later the typeface was adopted for the original Tumblr logo (2007–2013) by designer Peter Vidani — prior to Yahoo! acquisition mid-2013. Bookman Old Style was chosen here for its legibility, classic storybook styling, and general good humor.

www.ingramcontent.com/pod-product-compliance
Lightning Source LLC
Chambersburg PA
CBHW071813200626
46813CB00020B/2260